THE SPA

AN EROTIC ADVENTURE

VICTORIA RUSH

VOLUME 26

JADE'S EROTIC ADVENTURES - BOOK 26

COPYRIGHT

FEEL THE RUSH:

Jade's Erotic Adventures – Book 1

When lonely divorcée Jade seeks to broaden her horizons, she's invited to a private dinner event which promises to stimulate all of her senses. Wearing nothing but masquerade masks, dinner guests receive special service under the table while their fellow diners look on...

The Dinner Party

Jade's Erotic Adventures - Book 2

Jade discovers an exotic adventure club where strangers meet to explore each other's bodies in mysterious dark rooms. Using special effects to project swirling light patterns onto their figures, the shifting shadows provide just enough illumination to highlight their naked bodies while protecting their identities...

The Dark Room

Jade's Erotic Adventures - Book 3

Jade discovers a yoga club where members stretch and explore each other's bodies in the buff. She books an appointment, and during the first session meets a young redhead who tantalizes her with her flexibility and stunning body...

Naked Yoga

For the uninhibited...

1
___

"**W**hat's up, girl?" my best friend Hannah said to me at our weekly lunch date. "You look a little run down. Have you been taking care of yourself?"

"I've been going to yoga class as often as I can, and I think I'm eating reasonably well. But I've kind of been flitting from one empty relationship to another, and I guess I'm in a bit of a rut."

"Mmm," Hannah nodded. "Maybe you need to break away from your routine for a change. You know, mix up the scenery, go somewhere you can relax and recharge your batteries."

"What did you have in mind?" I said.

"I've been thinking," she smiled with a slight curl of her lip. "I've heard about this new spa in town that takes a different slant on the whole wellness concept."

"How so?"

"Well, for one thing, it's for ladies only."

"That's nothing new. Ninety-five percent of the clientele at most spas is already women."

"This one's on the top floor of one of the tallest skyscrapers in Chicago. It's got a retractable roof and a beautiful open-air patio surrounding a huge pool with magnificent views of the city and the lake."

"That *does* sound a little more upscale than most," I nodded. "But if that's its big claim to fame, I'm not sure that's going to be enough to pull me out of my funk."

"What if I told you it's a *naked* spa?"

"What do you mean?" I said, suddenly intrigued. "You mean customers receive facials and massages in the nude?"

"Well yes, but it's much more than that. I mean *everybody's* naked, including in the common areas like the pool, sauna, and exercise studio."

"Really? Like a nudist camp or something?"

"A very *elite* nudist camp," she smiled. "With all the spa amenities. Where everybody is super wellness-oriented and in fabulous shape. Imagine sitting poolside watching all the hot women going in and out of the pool and cavorting in the hot tub."

I shifted unsteadily on my chair, suddenly realizing how wet my panties had become envisioning the scenario.

"Is there a *lot* of cavorting going on?"

"Let's just say it's a voyeur's paradise, where women are encouraged to mingle. From what I've heard, it's Chicago's answer to Plato's Retreat. There's allegedly a ton of extra-curricular activities going on. Don't tell me that doesn't get your juices going."

"Um–*yeah*," I said, feeling my pussy throb at the idea of an all-girls venue. "That does sound a little different. What about the staff? They don't have a problem with all that lewd socializing?"

"Quite the opposite. Apparently, they're just as involved in the delivery of the special services. Can you imagine getting a full-body massage with a hot masseuse with all the extra benefits? Or a Brazilian, or a pedicure, or a facial where they make sure you're satisfied in *every* possible way?"

I leaned back in my chair, scrunching up my face.

"Don't you think it would be kind of weird getting a wax where the aesthetician is focused on more than just cleaning things up down there?"

"You never know until you try," Hannah said. "Come on, Jade–you deserve to be pampered for a change. This is a place you can go where there's no judging, no expectations, no relationship pressures. You can indulge as little or as much as you wish in the carnal opportunities. Or just lie in the sun, go for a dip in the pool, and take in the scenery."

"The very *erotic* scenery," I smiled.

"That never stopped you before," she said, arching an eyebrow.

"Okay," I said. "You've twisted my arm. When did you have in mind for this little excursion?"

"Tomorrow at noon," she said, holding up two tickets. "I've already paid for both of us. My treat."

"Are you planning to be my wingwoman to keep me out of trouble?"

"Fuck *that*," Hannah chuckled. "I'm going to be your *partner-in-crime*, to make sure you get into as much trouble as possible."

2

———

The following day, I met Hannah in the lobby of an office tower on Magnificent Mile. It was a beautiful sunny day, and I could see all the way down Grand Avenue toward the Navy Pier and Lake Michigan. I was ready to forget my troubles and lose myself in the luxury and decadence of the upscale spa. I had no idea what I was in for, but the throbbing in my pussy suggested it would be anything but boring.

"So, are you ready for this?" Hannah said while we waited for the elevator on the ground floor.

"I think so," I said. "My *mind* isn't so sure, but my body seems to have other ideas."

We stepped into the lift and Hannah nodded, tapping the button for the sixty-third floor.

"I'm just as excited as you are to see what this is all about. My mind's been racing with all the possibilities ever since I bought the tickets."

"You had this planned for me all along, didn't you?" I said.

"Of course," Hannah smirked. "How could I not invite my bestie to the hottest show in town?"

When the elevator reached the top floor and the doors opened, I saw a pretty attendant dressed in a blue uniform sitting behind a frosted-glass desk flanked by a streaming water wall.

"It's impressive looking, that's for sure," I said. "But I thought you said all the staff were naked?"

"They have to present a professional face to the general public," Hannah said. "But I assure you, once we get behind the reception area, it will be an entirely different picture. Come on, let's check this place out."

We strolled up to the front counter, and the attendant looked up from her computer screen.

"Good afternoon," the girl said. "How can I be of service?"

"We have two day-passes," Hannah said, sliding the tickets over the counter.

"Of course," the girl said, peering at the tickets. "You're welcome to use all of our club's features at your leisure. There's the pool of course, the outdoor patio, the hot tub, sauna, and exercise studio. But if you wish to avail yourselves of the special services, you'll have to make an appointment."

"What services do you offer, specifically?"

"Our aestheticians and massage therapists provide facials, manicures/pedicures, massages, and intimate grooming."

Hannah turned toward me and smiled.

"What do you think, Jade? What would you like to do first?"

"I think I'm pretty good with the grooming. How about a massage?"

I looked toward the attendant.

"Do you offer doubles massages? When's your next opening?"

"We do," she said. "Our therapists are just finishing up with another appointment. They should be available in about twenty minutes if you'd both like to give it a try."

"Yes, thank you," Hannah nodded.

The attendant handed each of us a card key to enter the premises and separate locker keys.

"The change room is through the door to the left. Each of the service areas is clearly marked. The massage therapists will be waiting for you at one p.m."

"Is there a particular dress code while traveling about the common areas?" Hannah asked.

"You'll find a terrycloth robe in each of your lockers and two large bath towels. You're welcome to wear either of these in the common areas or nothing at all, if you prefer. We want you to feel as relaxed and comfortable as possible at all times. Most of our guests choose to relax in the nude, as they find that most liberating."

Liberating, indeed, I smiled at the attendant, noticing a gleam in her eye.

Hannah and I took our keys and passed through the locked guest door, then followed the signs to the change room. When we got there, there was a handful of women coming in and out of the showers, making little effort to conceal their naked bodies. Most of them looked to be in their twenties and early thirties, with well-toned figures and golden-brown skin.

"Looks like we're going be the old ladies of the bunch," Hannah chuckled, opening her locker next to mine.

"I'm okay with that," I said, taking off my clothes and hanging them in the locker next to the robe. "If this is any indication of what the rest of the customers look like, that'll work for me. Besides, we're no slouches. I think we can hold our own against the competition."

Hannah peered at a pretty blonde giving her the eye as she bent over to step out of her pants.

"Something tells me there's going to be a *lot* of holding our own against these ladies before the day is over," she winked.

I glanced at a slim African-American girl emerging from one of the showers. She had flawless caramel-colored skin and a model-perfect figure with firm, high breasts, a narrow waist, and an exquisitely rounded ass. As she patted her short afro dry, I stole a glance between her legs, watching the water drip down over her bald, brown mound.

"Jesus," I said. "I could jump any one of these girls right now. I hope these ladies are just getting *started* their spa treatment, not finishing."

"Not to worry," Hannah smiled, noticing me drooling at the pretty black girl. "I'm pretty sure there's lots more where those came from. Just try to keep your dick in your pants for a little longer while we ease our way into this experience."

"Whatever you say, boss," I said. "So what's the protocol? Do we wear our robes into the massage room or traipse around in the buff like everyone else it seems to be doing?"

"I don't see any harm in wearing the robe to start," Hannah said. "Besides, we need *somewhere* we store our locker keys."

"Come on," she said, glancing at her phone screen before placing it on the locker shelf and locking the door. "It's time for our massage."

I followed Hannah down the hall to the waiting area for the massages, where we sat in the plush chairs, picking up two copies of Vogue magazine lying on the adjacent tables. As I began leafing through the glamour shots of the gorgeous models, I wondered how many of them had frequented this place. The African-American girl I saw in the change room certainly could have qualified for any of these shoots, and I felt my nipples hardening at the idea of engaging with her later. After a few minutes, the door to the massage room opened and a nude brunette girl approached us.

She had a more athletic figure than the black girl from the locker room, but was equally stunning. With large, round tits and a perfectly toned stomach and bare midriff, my pussy began watering just looking at her.

"Are you Hannah and Jade for the one o'clock massage appointment?"

"Um, yes," I stammered, momentarily taken aback by her casual attitude and Amazonesque figure.

"Please," she said. "Come in."

When we entered the room, I saw a second attendant leaning over a sink washing her hands as her tight ass flexed over rippling hamstrings and calves. I looked at Hannah with wide eyes, mouthing the words *Holy Shit!* She peered back at me with an equally incredulous look, shrugging her shoulders.

"Just go with the flow, baby," she whispered.

In the middle of the room rested two side-by-side massage tables about four feet apart, covered with a long bath sheet and a rolled-up towel resting in the middle section.

"Can we hang your robes for you?" the brunette said as the blonde attendant turned around, drying her hands.

She was even more beautiful than the brunette, with long silky hair tied up in a bun and a slender figure with the most exquisite tits I'd seen in a long time. With her compact round ass, long slender legs, and mouth-wateringly curvy hips, she had the figure of a twenty-year-old stripper. I could feel the moisture rapidly building up between my legs as a trickle of lubrication dripped down the inside of my thigh.

"By all means," Hannah said, practically throwing her robe at the attendant.

"Make yourselves comfortable on the massage tables, facing face-down," the brunette said, obviously the more experienced of the two girls.

When I lay down on one of the benches, I was happy when I saw the blonde girl approach my table with a bottle of massage oil. I would have been happy to have either girl touch me, but there was something about the blonde one that got my juices flowing. As I watched the brunette hovering over Hannah's naked body pouring oil into her hands, I glanced at Hannah with wide eyes. Neither of us had to say a word, since both of us were thinking the same thing. This was as close to heaven as two living and breathing people surely could have gotten.

When I felt the blonde's slippery hands run up my spine starting from the small of my back, at first I flinched from the unexpected sensation. But after she began softly pressing her thumbs and fingers into my muscles, I slowly relaxed, flitting my eyes in sublime bliss. Normally, I closed my eyes when I got a massage, concentrating on the relaxing feeling of my masseuse's fingers kneading my body. But with Hannah lying right next to me being serviced by a gorgeous Amazon, I kept them wide open, following her every movement and muscle twitch.

As she pressed her fingers into Hannah's back and slid her hands up and down her spine, I watched her tits jiggling and the muscles in her arms and stomach flexing. Her lower body was partially obscured by Hannah's prone figure, but that didn't stop me from dreaming about slipping my fingers into her bare snatch and licking her like a puppy dog. When the girls moved around to opposite sides of our tables revealing their bare asses for both of us to see, Hannah and I looked at one another again with wide eyes.

As I watched the front of my masseuse's body tensing and flexing only inches away from me, it took every ounce of my willpower not to reach out from the side of my table and touch her bald pussy. The more she caressed me, the more worked up I got watching the two girls' asses wiggling mere inches apart, and my hips began to squirm atop the rolled towel pressing into my pubis.

Just when I thought I couldn't take it any longer, the two masseuses moved to the other end of our bodies and began pressing their fingers into our calves, slowly working their way up our legs along the insides of our thighs. When the blonde girl reached the base of my buttocks, she stopped just short of my dripping slit then rolled her hands over my buttocks, squeezing them firmly. I pressed my mound down hard on the bumpy towel, desperately trying to give my aching clit some direct friction.

Feeling my buttocks flexing in her hands and sensing my rising tension, she swept her hands around the sides of my ass, cupping my cheeks with her thumbs pointed toward my fluttering pussy. I spread my legs further apart, inviting her to move her hand closer, and I gasped when she began running her thumbs up and down the sides of my slippery folds.

God yes, I thought, feeling my heart beginning to pound in my chest. *That's where I need your touch right now.*

I glanced over at Hannah, who had an equally intense look on her face as her attendant leaned over, caressing her vulva. I could see the slit of her masseuse's pussy between her round globes, and my eyes darted back and forth between the view of the blonde's bare mound moving inches away from my face and the brunette's inviting pussy glistening in the bright light of the massage room on the other side of Hannah's table.

I peered over at Hannah with my mouth agape and whispered *Thank You*. She simply smiled back at me and nodded knowingly. Something told me she knew exactly what she'd gotten us into, but at this precise moment I couldn't care less about her devious plan. Suddenly, the blonde girl adjusted her position with her left hand rested atop the base of my spine, while her other hand curled under my cheeks, penetrating my hole. When I felt her fingers enter my tunnel, I groaned, tilting my ass higher in the air.

Now I knew what the rolled-up towel was intended for. It was obviously meant to give the masseuses easier access to our undercarriage for this express purpose. As I began to roll my hips in concert with the blonde's probing of my pussy, I felt a stream of oil drip onto my buttocks, flowing down the crack of my ass over my rosebud and her dripping hand, now firmly embedded in my cunt. When I felt her other hand slide down over my ass and begin to massage my pucker, I groaned loudly and closed my eyes.

I was no longer interested in seeing what the other girl was doing to Hannah. I just wanted to concentrate on the heavenly sensation being administered by my own masseuse. When she began flicking my clit with the two little fingers of her right hand while she stimulated the walls of my pussy with her other fingers, I couldn't contain my pleasure any longer.

"Oh God," I moaned, fucking her hands with my ass and my pussy. My entire perineum from my asshole down to my clit was being simultaneously stimulated by the most sexy woman I'd seen in a long time.

"Yes," I purred, opening my eyes to see Hannah equally glazed over as her masseuse ministered to her in a similar manner.

I wondered if the couples' massage was designed to provide each of us simultaneous attention so we could arc through our pleasure in tandem. But at this point I hardly cared, as I surrendered to the mounting pleasure building inside me. Hannah and I peered at each other's faces while we read our bodies, knowing exactly what was happening to each other as we watched our reactions. We raised our arms over our heads and gripped the top of our padded tables tightly with our hands, and our mouths began to gape open as a flush rolled over each of our cheeks.

"Oh fuck," I groaned, feeling my orgasm beginning to pulse through me as my whole body began to shake. As I began clamping down on the blonde's fingers inside my pussy, she slipped her oiled thumb into my pucker while she fucked both of my holes as I writhed in delirious pleasure on the massage table.

"Uhnnn," Hannah groaned as I watched her ass quivering in the throes of her own powerful climax. The sight of the two gorgeous masseuse's fucking us with both hands while their bodies tensed and writhed overtop of our prone bodies was the most erotic thing I'd experienced in ages.

Hannah and I trembled and moaned on the massage tables for what seemed like an eternity, then our bodies both fell limp as our climaxes receded. For the first time in a long time, I felt completely relaxed and satisfied.

Maybe this spa idea wasn't such a bad idea after all, I smiled toward Hannah lying on the table next to me.

3

fter Hannah and I recovered from our dual massages, we headed to the pool to relax. The view of the city from the rooftop patio was magnificent, but the view *inside* was even more heart-stopping. Scores of naked women paraded in and out of the pool, while another group giggled inside an oversize, bubbling Jacuzzi. With the glass roof retracted, the bright overhead sun reflected off their glistening skin like sequins on their bare bodies.

We found two lounge chairs facing the shallow end of the pool and lay our bath towels on the padded cushions, then propped up the seatbacks so we'd have a good view of the action. The shallow end had descending steps leading into the basin, so we had a front-row seat for viewing the women as they slunk in and out of the water. As I watched the procession of beauties emerging from the pool dripping in erotic sensuality, I squeezed my thighs together trying to quiet my burning clit.

"You weren't kidding about this place being a voyeur's paradise," I chuckled to Hannah.

"Tell me about it," she said. "I can't decide if I prefer them coming or going."

"I could come again watching them either way. Is *everybody* in this place drop-dead gorgeous with model-perfect figures?"

"Well, it *is* the city's most exclusive spa, so I guess these girls know how to take care of themselves. But I also suspect a lot of it has to do with the fact that they know they're going to be under a microscope traipsing around in the nude. Maybe only the prettiest ones feel confident enough to flaunt their bodies so openly."

"Don't get me wrong," I said. "I'm definitely enjoying the show. It's just that I haven't felt this self-conscious about my body in a long time."

Hannah cocked her head toward me, peering over the top of her sunglasses.

"Don't sell yourself short, girl. You're just as pretty and sexy as any one of these hot mamas. Maybe you should get out there and do a little flaunting of your own."

"Perhaps in a little while," I said. "Right now, I'm just happy to do the watching."

"So are you glad I twisted your arm to come up here?" she said, lying back in her chair to soak up the sun.

"Definitely. This is even more dreamy than I imagined."

"And did you enjoy your massage?"

"Couldn't you tell? I think my masseuse probed every one of my erogenous zones."

"That's what I call a *full-body* massage," Hannah smiled.

"I was kind of hoping they'd flip us over afterward and get on top of us to complete the procedure. I don't know about you, but I had a hard time resisting the temptation to reach out and grope them as they moved around the table."

"I suspect that was all by design," Hannah nodded. "To build up our excitement for the big finish."

"That was a hell of a happy ending. I haven't come that hard in months."

"And we're just getting started," Hannah smiled. "Think of all the opportunities to connect in this place."

Suddenly, I noticed the pretty black girl from the locker room emerge from the outside patio and begin to walk in our direction.

"Oh, I'm *thinking*, alright," I said, pushing myself higher in my chair to get a better view.

Hannah followed my line of sight toward the girl and smiled.

"Isn't that the same girl you were eyeballing in the change room? She seems to be just as interested in you as you were in her."

As she moved closer toward us, we made eye contact, checking each other's figures out.

"I dunno, Han," I said. "I think she's out of my league. She looks like an African goddess."

"Well it appears that she's going to give us a bird's-eye view of her figure at least. Maybe she'll take a dip in the pool, where we can get a closer look at her."

As the girl walked toward the shallow end of the pool, I watched her tits jiggling on her chest and her long leg muscles flexing. When she got within a few feet of us, she turned toward the turquoise water and paused at the top of the steps. Her backside was even more spectacular than her front, with her swelling hips and a perfectly round ass accentuating her tawny, hourglass figure.

"Fuck me," I whispered to Hannah, peering down the crack of her ass toward the dark folds showing between her slightly parted thighs.

"That could be arranged if you play your cards right," she chuckled.

After a few seconds, the girl stepped into the water, slowly immersing her body into the sparkling surf. Then she leaned forward and began swimming toward the other end using a graceful breast stroke. As her legs flapped in and out, I watched her sexy ass rising and falling under the surface while the water swirled over her caramel body.

"Oh my God," I panted. "*Pinch* me to make sure I'm not dreaming."

"It's not a dream, babe," Hannah smiled. "That is one sexy-ass, flesh-and-blood woman."

"Just when I thought it couldn't possibly get any hotter than those two masseuses that worked us over. I'd take *this* one over three of them in a heartbeat."

When the girl reached the other end of the pool, she flipped over onto her other side and began swimming with a backstroke toward us. While her arms slowly windmilled through the water, her body rolled from side to side as the water washed over her sensuous breasts like waves on a beach. The closer she got to me, the more my heart raced, imagining her swimming right into my moistening lap.

"Yes, sweetheart," I purred, spreading my legs apart. "Dock yourself right here."

Hannah and I sat mesmerized watching her sylphlike figure slicing through the water, until one of her hands tapped the steps in the shallow end. Then she turned around and walked out of the water directly in front of us, smiling as she made eye contact with me. I couldn't help running my eyes over the front of her dripping body as my legs twitched involuntarily. Then she turned and retraced her steps around the perimeter of the pool, reclining in a vacant lounge chair at the opposite end.

"Did you see how she looked at you?" Hannah said, peering over at me. "She was practically fucking you with her eyes."

"I hardly noticed, watching the rest of her incredible body."

"I think you need to take advantage of this opportunity while the iron is still hot," she said. "Why don't you go over there and introduce yourself?"

"I wouldn't exactly say that was a green light to go hit on her. I don't want to intrude on her privacy if she just wants some peace and quiet."

"Well then, why don't you give her some of her own medicine by parading your body up and down the pool for everyone else to see? Let's see if she takes the bait."

"I don't know if *bait* is the right metaphor in this case, but I'd be thrilled if she gobbled me up right about now. I could use a refreshing dip in the pool anyways. After that hot massage session and watching that nymph take a sexy bath, I need to cool off. Hold my chair for me?"

"I wouldn't dream of giving it away. You go girl, go get your Lorelei."

I raised myself up from my chair then walked up to the edge of the shallow end and paused, peering across the reflecting surface hoping to catch the girl watching me from the other end of the pool. Although I was a little more full-figured than her, I maintained a tight, yoga-toned physique, with full, perky breasts, a flat stomach, and curvy hips. My pussy throbbed at the thought of her ogling me as I had with her.

While I lowered myself into the water, I kept my gaze pointed down, pretending to ignore her. Mimicking her lead, I began swimming breast strokes in her direction, with my head bobbing in and out of the water. When I neared the far wall, I glanced up at her chair resting near the edge of the pool and noticed her legs were slightly parted and she had a sexy smile on her face.

Jesus, I thought, touching the wall right in front of her. *Was she signaling her interest in me the same way I had earlier?*

As I turned around, I couldn't help smiling at our sexy cat-and-mouse game, then I pushed back from the wall floating on my back, using a reverse breast stroke technique. While I flapped my legs slowly in and out, I lifted my ass to the surface of the water, letting her watch the churning surf rising and falling over my exposed bare pussy. As I swung my arms slowly behind me, I glanced at the side of the pool and noticed that all the women were staring at my breasts poking out of the water.

Good, I thought. *Maybe if the African-American girl sees that I'm attracting the attention of some of the other pretty women, she'll make the next move.*

When I reached the shallow end, I walked up the stairs slowly so the girl on the other end could watch my round ass dripping with moisture. Then I lay down on my lounge chair next to Hannah, not even bothering to dry off.

"Holy shit, girl," she said. "I think you might have just one-upped your African goddess. Every set of eyes in the room was watching you as you swam across both lengths of the pool. You even got *me* going with that performance. If that doesn't pull her toward you like a magnet, I don't know what will."

I turned my head to gaze in the black girl's direction and noticed she was walking back toward our end once again.

"See?" Hannah said. "You've obviously tweaked her interest. Let's see if she says hello."

As the girl moved closer toward us, I could feel my pussy throbbing, but when she reached the end of the pool, she glimpsed at me briefly then continued on to the end of the platform, disappearing into the sauna room.

"*Well?*" Hannah said, peering at me with raised eyebrows. "What are you waiting for? That's an invitation if I ever saw one."

"Yeah?" I said, still not convinced. "Are you sure?"

"She was watching you the entire walk back toward our end of the pool. Then she goes into a private room in full view of you. I don't think you need a crystal ball to know that she wants you."

"Okay," I said. "Should I bring a towel or something to cover up?"

"Was *she* wearing a towel?" Hannah said sarcastically.

"Fine. But if I'm not out in twenty minutes, come check up on me to make sure I haven't passed out or something. I'm feeling so light-headed right now, I'm afraid all that hot steam might make me collapse at the knees."

"I'm quite sure you won't need any help from me," she said. "But if she happens to come out first and I don't see any sign of you within a few minutes, I'll make sure you haven't fainted from all the pleasure you're about to receive."

"Wish me luck," I said, slowly rising from my chair, trying not to make it too obvious to everybody else in the room that I was following the girl into the sauna.

When I got to the room, I swung open the door and saw her sitting on the upper bunk with her left knee propped up on the bench, exposing her pink slit. Another woman rested on the bench directly beneath her, leaning back against the wood planks with her hands resting by her sides. I took a position kitty-corner to them on the lower bench, then leaned back against the wall with my opposite leg propped up, concealing my pussy.

I lay my head back and closed my eyes, pretending to

relax and enjoy the hot steam. But when I opened them briefly and peered in the black girl's direction, I saw her right hand positioned in front of her pussy, moving her fingers in slow circles below her mound.

Holy shit, I thought. *She's playing with herself in full view of me!*

At first, I was so shocked at her brazen act of exhibitionism that I looked away, thinking she wanted to watch me only when she knew I wasn't looking. But when I peered back at her a few moments later, her legs were spread even further apart, exposing her beautiful pink vulva against her chocolate-brown skin. As her hand began to move in faster circles over her clit, her mouth parted open and I could hear her panting softly.

I glanced down at the other woman sitting below her who still had her eyes closed, oblivious to the ministrations of the sexy girl sitting directly above her. Feeling the sticky juices building up between my legs, I lowered my right hand into my lap and began rubbing my clit behind my propped-up leg. I didn't feel comfortable exposing myself fully in case the other woman opened her eyes, but I gazed directly back at the black girl as we massaged our clits.

As I began to feel the sweat dripping over my forehead and the pleasure spreading throughout my body, I slowly lowered my raised leg and spread my thighs apart, showing the girl my dripping pussy. She grabbed one of her tits with her free hand and pinched her long nipple while she stared at my glistening snatch. Before long, both of us were moaning softly, jilling ourselves with increasing fervor.

When I glanced down at the other woman to make sure it was still safe, I was surprised to see that she also had her legs spread apart and was rubbing her pussy as she watched me playing with myself. But at this point, I was too far gone to stop what I was doing, and knowing that the we were all aligned with our intentions, I began to moan and twist my hips on the warm cedar bench. When the black girl thrust her hand inside her pink folds and began thumping her back against the wall in rising pleasure, I couldn't resist the temptation any longer.

I rose from my bench and walked directly in front of her, positioning my head between her legs, then I pulled her hips hard into my face, eating her pussy like it was my last meal. She placed her hands behind my head and pulled me toward her, squeezing my head between her powerful thighs. As I reached up to grab her tits, I felt the woman's hand from below probing my slit, then she placed two fingers thrust inside me. While I moaned into the black girl's cunt, I lifted one foot and placed it on the bench beside the other woman and I felt her lips suck my erect clit into her mouth.

With my face buried in the black girl's snatch and my own pussy being serviced from below, I moaned into her cleft, feeling my orgasm approaching like a freight train. When it slammed into me, I groaned loudly into the girl's pussy, and she grabbed my hair while she clamped her thighs tightly against the sides of my head, quivering on the edge of the bench.

She held me in this clenched position for so long I was afraid she might suffocate me, but I dared not come up for air while she was in the throes of a powerful orgasm. After many long seconds, she finally loosened her grip and relaxed her legs then she leaned forward, thrusting her tongue into my dripping mouth. As we kissed each other passionately, the woman below removed her fingers from my pussy and I heard the sound of her breathing beginning to escalate while she attended to her own needs.

For the entire time the three of us were in the sauna, none of us had said a single word to one another. I didn't even know the *name* of the girl whose cunt I'd just finished eating out. There was something about this anonymous, no-strings-attached, down-and-dirty spa that I was digging. It didn't look like Hannah would have to save me after all.

For the first time since entering the spa, I felt completely liberated, ready to explore all the carnal opportunities on my own.

4

Feeling a bit awkward after my fling in the sauna, I left the room soon after and headed back over to my spot by the pool. I saw Hannah taking a leisurely swim, so I headed over to the juice bar and picked up two smoothies. When I returned to my lounge chair, I glanced around the room, soaking up the scene. With so many sexy women prancing around the place, I was surprised more of them weren't hooking up.

Maybe they're just self-conscious about making out in public, I thought. *Or maybe they're waiting for someone to break the ice.*

I glanced over in the direction of the hot tub, noticing a small group of women chatting and laughing in the bubbly froth.

If that's not the perfect place for a little extra-curricular activity, I don't know what is.

Hannah emerged from the pool and walked toward me, wringing out her hair.

"*So?*" she smiled. "How did it go in there? Did you finally get your freak on with your African goddess?"

"It definitely got pretty hot," I nodded.

"Like, almost *pass-out* hot? I'm a little disappointed you didn't call for reinforcements. Try as I might to attract the attention of other women in this place, everybody seems to be ignoring me."

I glanced at Hannah's naked body, admiring her tight, shapely figure. There was no reason she shouldn't be connecting with other girls, and I felt a little guilty for abandoning her.

"Maybe you just need a little extra *lubricant*," I said. "The hot tub in the corner looks like it might be more conducive for some close-quarter mingling. Do you want to give it a go?"

"Sure," Hannah said. "But don't you need a little time to recover? What happened to your girlfriend?"

"It seems she was only interested in one thing," I shrugged. "But I *could* use a little rest."

I pointed to the tall glass resting on the table beside Hannah's chair.

"I brought you a smoothie. Why don't we cool off before jumping back into the fire?"

Hannah patted her hair dry with a towel then lay back in her chair, taking a sip of her smoothie.

"So, have you had your eye on anyone *else* in this place?"

"Not really," I said. "Just about everybody looks seriously fuckable. I wouldn't mind wrapping my legs around that cute blonde masseuse though, if I had a chance. But I'm guessing that's against the rules."

"I dunno. What's good for the goose is good for the gander, in a manner of speaking. Maybe you just need to get her alone someplace."

"Perhaps I can schedule a *one-on-one* massage next time," I said. "I'm pretty sure I could persuade her to participate in a more interactive session if I had her all to myself."

"So you're thinking of coming *back*, then?" Hannah smiled. "Have they got you hooked already?"

"It's pretty hard to ignore a place like this," I nodded. "I wonder if they have monthly memberships?"

"The amenities would seem to fit that model. It's almost like more of a *health club*, with a few extra perks. Albeit some pretty fucking *awesome* perks."

"Speaking of," I said, peering over in the direction of the girls in the hot tub. "Are you ready to check out some of those other amenities?"

"Absolutely," she smiled. "If I can't hook up with someone there, at least I should be able to get some *other* kind of stimulation in the Jacuzzi."

We picked up our unfinished smoothies and carried them over toward the hot tub. When we got there, I noticed there were already four women submerged in the bubbling water and I wondered if there'd be enough room for Hannah and me.

"Have you got room for two more?" I asked.

"Absolutely," one of the girls said. "The more the merrier."

The women pressed their bodies closer together, and Hannah and I scooched in next to them. The water was warmer than I expected, but it didn't take long for me to get used to it, especially with the fleshy bodies of the other women rubbing up next to me.

"I haven't seen you guys here before," a forty-something redhead said, smiling at me. "First time visiting our spa?"

"Yes," I said.

"What do you think so far?"

"It's definitely a different kind of experience," I nodded, not yet ready to reveal just how *much* I'd actually enjoyed it.

"Have you availed yourself of any of the special services yet?" she said.

"Hannah and I had a couples massage a little while ago. It was very invigorating."

"Yes, those masseuses really know how to pinpoint the right spots," she smiled. "I'm Amber by the way."

I scanned her pretty face, admiring her piercing green eyes and high cheekbones. Although she was slightly older than most of the other women in the spa, she was equally as stunning, reminding me of the pretty runway model, Angie Everhart.

"Jade," I said. "And this is–"

"Hannah," Amber nodded. "Nice to see some fresh meat in this place, what do you think girls?" She peered around her, nodding at the other women in the tub, roughly her same age. "This is Kat, Anna, and Tammy."

"So are you guys–" I said, wondering if they came here often.

"Old fogies?" Amber laughed. "Yeah, I guess you could say we're regulars. There's more than *one* way to stay young at heart, you know."

"Speaking of," her friend Kat smiled. "We noticed you and that pretty black girl checking each other out earlier. Were you finally able to consummate your little courtship in the sauna?"

"Um..."

"It's okay," Amber chuckled. "We know *everything* that goes on in this place. Why else would we have lifetime memberships?"

I huffed softly, not quite sure how to respond.

"So are you two–?" Amber said, glancing at Hannah.

"No," Hannah said, shaking her head. "We're just good friends."

"That's a shame, because you look like a perfect match. Two pretty girls, one a blonde, the other a brunette. What are you, like barely *thirty*?"

"That's very generous," Hannah chuckled. "Just a little north of that. Maybe this invigorating spa treatment is beginning to work it's wonders already."

"There's a good chance. But you look like you could use a little extra stimulation. While your girlfriend's been improving her circulation in the steam room, you've been left to your own devices. There's a special spot over here where you can have some extra fun if you want."

"Oh?" Hannah said, suddenly perking up.

"I've been sitting right in front of it this whole time. Would you like to give it a try?"

"Sure," Hannah said, happy to have attracted the attention of some other women finally.

"Come," Amber said, standing up in the pool. "Let's switch positions. You come sit over here next to Kat and I'll sit next to your pretty girlfriend."

While Hannah and Amber switched positions, I took a moment to check out Amber's body. She had plump breasts with surprising firmness for her age and well-toned arms with tight, supple skin. Her wet hair draped over her lightly speckled chest and with her flushed cheeks and erect nipples, I found myself unconsciously spreading my legs trying to increase the flow of swirling water over my throbbing pussy.

When Hannah sat in her vacated spot, Kat suddenly reached under the water, pulling her legs forward a few inches, and Hannah's face lit up.

"*Right?*" Amber smiled, pressing her body up next to me. "I told you you'd like it. There's nothing like an invigorating water jet massage directed to the perfect location. Are you feeling more comfortable now?"

"Oh *yes*," Hannah grunted, shifting her hips closer to the pulsating underwater stream. "This is way better than the usual sex toys I'm accustomed to."

"And the best part is there's no *cleanup* required afterward. You can get off and freshen up at the same time."

"Mmm," Hannah moaned, surrendering to the feeling of the powerful spray stimulating her clit.

Suddenly Kat turned her body toward her and reached under the water, caressing her tits.

"Uhnn," Hannah groaned, turning her face toward Kat as they began kissing.

"Now *that's* a beautiful sight, don't you agree, Jade?"

"Absolutely," I hummed. "This is just what Hannah needed."

Amber placed her hand under the water and extended her arm toward my crotch. When she felt my fingers moving softly over my clit, she lowered her hand a few inches lower, thrusting two fingers into my hole. I didn't know what it was about this place, but I didn't seem to mind the members taking these kinds of liberties with my body. Between the swirling water jets pounding against my hips and Amber's sexy body rubbing up against my breasts, I was more than ready to ramp things up.

"That's a nice tight cunny you have," Amber purred. "Shall I continue?"

"Yes please," I moaned, flitting my eyelids in pleasure.

Amber suddenly raised herself off the bench and turned around to face me, straddling my hips and pressing her mound into my stomach.

"Mmm," she purred, pressing her melons against my tits.

"You're *soft*, too. Do you like watching your girlfriend getting off under the water?"

"Yes," I panted.

With the four of us now actively engaged with each other, Tammy raised herself off her seat and sat down over Anna's thighs, facing the rest of us. Apparently, nobody except Amber wanted to miss catching the rest of the action in the hot tub while we groped and caressed one another.

Amber reached behind her back with her hand, cupping my trembling hand as I massaged my pussy. Then she placed three fingers inside me, fucking me while I stimulated my clit. She leaned in to kiss me, and I felt her hips tilt as she began rocking her pussy against the top of my mound. The idea of being fucked by this sexy older redhead while she rubbed her big tits against my breasts excited me tremendously, and before long we were tongue-fucking each other as we moaned into each other's mouths.

I peered over at Anna and Tammy, whose eyes were glazed over watching the rest of us as they rubbed their vulvas together with Anna squeezing her friend's tits from behind. Then I glanced over at Hannah and saw that Kat had angled her body toward her with one leg resting over her thigh, trying to get in on the powerful stream now pulsing toward both of their pussies. She smiled at me, nodding at how pleased she was with the turn of events.

With the heat in the hot tub beginning to ramp up, Amber and I began pressing our hips together more vigorously as our moans began rising in pitch in volume, and I could feel myself veering on the precipice, ready to pop off any second. Sensing I was close, Amber pressed her palm harder against my fluttering hand while she stroked my G-spot with her three fingers. Then she pressed her little finger further down my perineum until it rested against my pucker. While she moved her hand in circles overtop of mine, I spread my legs further apart, moaning loudly into her mouth.

"Yes," I grunted, feeling myself falling over the edge. "You're going to make me cum, Amber. *Oh my God–*"

As my orgasm washed over me, Amber pressed her little finger into my rosebud, and my entire perineum began clamping down over her hand.

"Yes, baby," she purred. "Let it go. Come for Momma."

I could feel her press her pussy more forcefully into my stomach as she rocked her hips with greater urgency, gripping my hips with her thighs.

"Uhnnn!" I cried, consumed with pleasure as I watched the other girls reaching their apex at the same time.

When the six of us finally stopping grunting and groaning, I looked around the spa and noticed that virtually everybody else in the poolroom had suddenly paired up, enjoying their own little moment of bliss.

5

———

After the wild ride in the hot tub, I needed some alone time, so I headed to the exercise studio to stretch and relax. Finding it empty, I walked over to a large padded mat against the far wall and sat down, pulling my hands toward my feet to loosen my leg muscles. The entire room was lined in floor-to-ceiling mirrors, with equal parts dedicated to aerobic classes, weight machines, and stretching. I remembered seeing aerobic classes on the list of services at the front desk, and I smiled at the thought of everybody's boobs bouncing up and down as they went through their paces.

No wonder everyone in this place is so fit and toned, I thought. There weren't many places in the spa where you could avoid being seen or seeing your own naked body from just about any angle. *There's virtually nowhere to hide or cover up.*

As I moved through my usual yoga poses on the mat, I watched myself in the mirror. I was proud of the tight figure I'd been able to maintain over the years, and I smiled seeing the muscles flexing in my arms and legs while I strained to hold the poses. But stretching in the buff was a whole *different* experience, and I felt my nipples hardening and my pussy moistening as I watched my tits and glistening vulva in the glass.

While I held my toes high off the mat balancing on my ass in a split-leg position, suddenly the door swung open and a familiar face entered the room. It was the pretty blonde from the massage room. She glanced at my exposed pussy reflecting in the mirror and smiled when I lowered my feet, closing my legs to protect my modesty.

"Don't stop on my account," she said, taking a position on the mat a few feet to my side. "A woman with your physique shouldn't be afraid to reveal every part of her glorious figure."

"Thanks," I said, leaning forward to rest my breasts on top of my thighs. "I didn't want to be too bold. I already feel exposed enough in this place as it is."

"You shouldn't feel self-conscious in here," she said. "That's the beauty of this spa. It's a place where women can go to free their minds and spirits without feeling judged in any way."

"It seems that's not the *only* thing that gets freed in this place," I smiled, alluding to our intimate session earlier in the day. "I had no idea I'd be releasing my inhibitions in so many different ways."

"*Jade*, isn't it?" she said, pinching her eyebrows together. "I remember you from this morning's massage."

"Yes," I said, blushing softly.

"I'm Julie," she said, reaching out to extend her hand. "We were never properly introduced."

"No, I suppose not," I said, feeling the hairs on my arms standing on end as I touched her for the first time. "I guess we were too preoccupied with other things."

"Mmm," she nodded. "Have you enjoyed your visit to our spa so far?"

"Oh yes," I said. "It's far surpassed my expectations. It's been a feast for the senses in so many ways. So much so that I needed to come in here and wind down for a few moments."

"I know what you mean," Julie said. "I like to come in here to stretch and meditate between appointments. I find it very therapeutic."

I watched her in the mirror as she twisted and contorted her body into increasingly difficult poses.

"How long have you been working here?"

"Only a couple of months. It's nice that the management allows us to use the facilities along with the rest of the members and guests."

As she moved through her stretches and poses, I marveled at her tight, lithesome figure. She was more slender than me, with smaller but firmer breasts and long, sinewy muscles that flexed sensuously as she went through her motions. When she leaned forward and lifted herself off the mat into a crow position, I admired her flexing arm muscles supporting her weight. But when she shifted into an inverted arm balance with her legs curved up over her shoulders, I couldn't help peering between her legs at her exposed slit.

"I always found that pose one of the tougher ones to hold," I said, feeling my pussy growing wetter by the moment.

"The key is to place your arms far enough apart with your legs positioned forward," she said. "Then slowly tilt your weight until you feel yourself balanced on your hands. Why don't you try it with me?"

She dropped her legs to the floor, then placed her hands and feet on the mat in a bent-over pose.

"You start in this position then gradually shift more of your weight over your hands. When you feel like you're supporting most of your weight on your arms, curl your legs forward and raise your feet off the floor."

I followed Julie's lead, panting heavily as I strained my arm muscles trying to support my weight.

"That's it," she nodded, seeing me raise my ass off the floor. "Now cross your ankles in front of your arms to lock yourself into position."

When I finally achieved the position, it felt surprisingly easy to hold the pose with everything held neatly together.

"That's excellent," Julie smiled. "It's not so difficult when you get into the right position, is it?"

"No," I puffed, staring at her pretty tits pressing together in the bent-over pose.

"Do you want to try something a little more challenging?" she asked.

"Okay," I said, feeling the cool air from below flowing over my exposed pussy.

"Keep your weight balanced over your arms, then unlock your ankles and extend your legs straight out in front of you until they're parallel with the floor."

I followed Julie's direction, grunting loudly as I felt the pressure building on my arms.

"Remember to keep your weight shifted forward so you don't fall back."

After a few seconds of struggling, I managed to achieve the pose, albeit with slightly crooked legs.

"That's fantastic, Jade," Julie said, peering at me in the mirror. "Why don't we take it one step further and see if we can shift into the firefly position."

Julie angled her legs higher in the air, tilting her ass toward the floor until her legs were pointed forty-five degrees up in the air, with her entire body balancing on her outstretched arms. With her pussy staring directly in front of me between her splayed legs, it took all of my concentration to stay focused on executing the technique.

"I'll try," I panted, feeling some drops of lubrication falling onto the mat between my legs.

With my legs pointing forward as much as I could, I slowly lowered my hips toward the floor, balancing my suspended weight over my arms until I matched the angle of Julie's upturned legs. I could feel the strain in my hamstrings from my legs pulled back behind my shoulders, and I glanced in the mirror, seeing the reflection of the bright overhead lights reflecting off my glistening, wet pussy.

"You got it, girl!" Julie said, peering between my legs. "How does it feel?"

"Strangely invigorating," I grunted, running my eyes all over Julie's body in front of me. "But this is killing my hamstrings. I think I need to loosen up a bit more before trying some of these more advanced poses."

"Absolutely," she nodded. "You don't want to hurt yourself. Let's give your muscles a rest before you pull something."

I lowered myself onto the mat then placed my hands beside my quivering legs, breathing heavily in and out.

"That was exhilarating," I said, peering over at Julie. "You've obviously got many talents beyond massage therapy."

"It's all part of the mind-body connection," she smiled. "Strength, flexibility, relaxation. It keeps us healthy in many different ways."

I glanced at her perfect tits glistening with sweat, feeling my pussy throbbing in excitement.

"If this is what it takes to achieve your level of fitness, I'm all in. I don't think I've seen another woman with as perfectly toned a figure as yours."

"You're no slouch yourself, Jade. It's just a matter of building up your stamina. Do you want to try some *partnered* stretching to loosen up your muscles a bit more?"

I'd been waiting for a chance to pair up with the pretty masseuse, and when she indicated she was ready to move to a new phase in our routine, I suddenly became aware of the puddle forming on the mat between my legs.

"As long as you promise not to twist me into a pretzel this time."

"No worries," she smiled. "This next one is super simple and far more relaxing. All you have to do is sit on the mat with your legs extended in front of you, with your feet spread apart a few inches. I'll face towards you with our feet touching together, then we can hold hands and gently pull each other forward and back to stretch the back of our leg muscles."

I nodded, imagining myself rocking back and forth with her in whole *different* kind of position.

Julie shifted her body around in front of me, and when she spread her legs and touched her feet to mine, I felt a surge of electricity coursing through me. I had to fight hard to keep my gaze above her neckline as she smiled and reached out her hands toward me.

"Now bend forward one inch at a time while I hold your arms. When you feel the tension in the back of your thighs, breathe deeply and try to relax until you feel the pressure receding."

I was able to bend forward far enough to clasp her hands, and I smiled when she squeezed me gently.

"Now, let me pull you slowly toward me until you feel tightness in your hamstrings again. Stop me when it begins to bind, then breathe slowly in and out until you feel your leg muscles relax."

I did as she instructed, and after a few minutes Julie was able to pull my upper body almost parallel with my legs resting on the floor.

"There you go," she nodded. "Now let's see if we can do the same thing with the adductor muscles on the inside of your thighs. I want you to spread your feet slowly apart as I maintain tension on your arms. You should feel pressure in the muscles on the side of your crotch as you begin to lengthen the tendons on the inside of your legs."

"I definitely feel *something* there," I huffed, watching the slit between Julie's legs open wider and wider the further I pressed my legs apart. She glanced between my thighs, noticing the wet spot on the mat directly in front of me.

"Remember to go slow," she said. "You definitely don't want to pull *this* muscle. This one's pretty important for maintaining sexual health and flexibility."

"You don't have to remind me twice about that one," I smiled. "I definitely don't want to put a damper on that."

"Okay, now lean back and begin to pull *me* forward now. This way we can *both* benefit from this stretch while we pump the blood through our muscles in this area."

"Yes," I purred, pulling her upper body toward me as we pressed our feet further apart. "I feel my circulation improving already."

The more we pulled our bodies toward one another, the further our legs pressed apart, bringing our pussies closer together and our bodies closer to touching. But just as her face moved to within inches of my throbbing snatch, the gym door swung open and two women paused at the entrance, seeing us in the compromising position.

"Do you mind if we join you?" one of the girls said, staring at the glistening reflection of my wet pussy.

"I'm good if you are, Jade," Julie said while I felt her breath inches away from my dripping pussy.

"Of course," I said, not wanting to throw a wet blanket on our fun. "There's lots of room on the mat for more people."

The girls sat down beside us, assuming a similar position.

"That stretch looks interesting," the first one said. "It certainly looks more stimulating than doing it alone."

"It's even more fun to perform it as a *group*," Julie said. "Why don't we form a circle with our feet touching and see if we can stretch and loosen our muscles *together*?"

She shifted her ass back a few inches then spread her legs further apart, inviting the girls into the circle. They positioned themselves next to us, then Julie spread her arm to her side, clasping the hand of the girl next to her. I did the same until we were all holding hands with our legs forty-five degrees apart, touching our feet in a chain-link circle.

"Well now that we're getting to know each other a little better," the first girl said. "I suppose we should introduce ourselves. I'm Taylor and this is Quinn."

"Pleased to meet you," Julie said. "I'm Julie."

"Jade," I said, nodding to each of the girls.

"So how does this work exactly?" Taylor said, glancing down at the juices coating the inside of my thighs.

"Jade and I were pulling each other to stretch our hamstrings and adductor muscles. But in a perfect circle, we'll be maintaining equal pressure between the four of us, so in order to move closer together, let's try spreading our legs further apart."

As we all followed Julie's instructions, our circle slowly began collapsing into a diamond shape.

"That's the idea," Julie said. "Can you girls feel the tension between your legs the closer we get to one another?"

"Yes, and that's not the *only* thing I'm feeling," Quinn said, glancing at our glistening pussies coming closer together.

"When we get close enough to our partners," Julie said, "reach out and clasp her hands, pulling you closer together. As you rock back and forth, you should be able to spread your feet further apart, slowly releasing the tension on the inside of your thighs."

"Mmm," Taylor groaned. "I feel it. How close should we try to get to one another?"

"As close as possible," Julie smiled. "If you can relax your adductors enough, ideally you should be able to touch in the middle."

As the four of us pulled each other closer and closer, spreading our legs further apart, Julie's upper body began to bend over my hips with her tits edging tantalizingly close to my throbbing pussy. I glanced at Taylor and Quinn, whose feet were pressed against the sides of Julie's and mine, and they smiled at each other as they peered between each of their open legs. Before long, both couple's glistening pussies were only inches apart as we pulled our upper bodies closer toward our hardening nipples and parted mouths. When I felt the strands of Julie's hair caress the top of my breasts, I pulled her harder toward me and she encircled one of my teats in her mouth.

"Mmm," I groaned, trying to spread my legs into a one-hundred-and-eighty-degree split, desperate to feel her pussy up against me.

But after a few moments, she began pulling me in the opposite direction. As I leaned forward over her tight abdomen, I licked my tongue up the crease in the center of her stomach until I reached the base of her tits. Then I sucked her medallions into my mouth, circling her nipples with my tongue, and she tilted her hips forward, touching our vulvas. I moaned loudly into her breasts when I felt our juices intermingling, but as soon as our clits touched, she suddenly leaned forward, pressing her body back in my direction.

I was beginning to go crazy with all this reciprocal teasing, wanting to feel Julie's lips against my own as we ground our pussies together. By now, all four of us had our legs spread into a virtual split, with the original circle collapsed into two parallel lines. Growing impatient, I pulled Julie hard toward me until her body rested on top of me, and she began kissing me as we rubbed our tits and vulvas together. This time, there was no desire for either of one of us to separate while we ground our wet pussies together, rubbing our hard clits over one another.

"Fuck yes," I purred into her mouth. "This is insanely hot. Rub your body against me, Julie."

"You've reached the height of your flexibility," she nodded. "Now just try to relax your muscles while you let the rest of your body enjoy the experience."

"Oh yes," I panted. "I'm definitely shifting my concentration to *other* parts of my body."

I peered at Taylor and Quinn out of the corner of my eye and saw that they were similarly commingled, rubbing their pussies and tits against one another with their legs spread wide apart.

"Uhhn," I heard them groan next to Julie and me.

There was something incredibly sexy about the four of us touching our feet together while we rubbed our bodies next to one another, listening to the mounting passion generated between the four of us. I tilted my head up a few inches and looked in the mirror in front of us. With Julie's legs splayed wide apart and our mounds joined together, I saw both of our slits spread open as our juices rolled down over each other's vulvas. I'd never seen anything so sexy in all my life, and the fact that we were engaged in a two-way affair with Taylor and Quinn right next to us just added to my excitement.

I began to feel the pleasure rising inside me and with our hands no longer needed to pull ourselves together, I wrapped my arms around Julie's back and thrust my tongue into her mouth, feeling my climax edging closer. When it finally hit me, I groaned loudly in Julie's mouth, spraying my juices over her vulva and ass while she grunted simultaneously inside my mouth. As the four of us writhed and groaned on the mat in simultaneous union, I heard some movement by the door and glanced up to see a large group of women pausing at the entrance, with their mouths wide agape.

It didn't take long for them to rush toward us joining us on the mat, rolling together in a giant heap of naked, writing bodies. As we intertwined our arms and legs, sucking and rocking against whatever body part presented itself to each of us, I smiled realizing I'd reached a new kind of nirvana. Something told me this spa was about to become my new go-to gym for the foreseeable future.

THE
DINNER
PARTY
AN EROTIC ADVENTURE
VICTORIA RUSH
Everybody's an exhibitionist in disguise

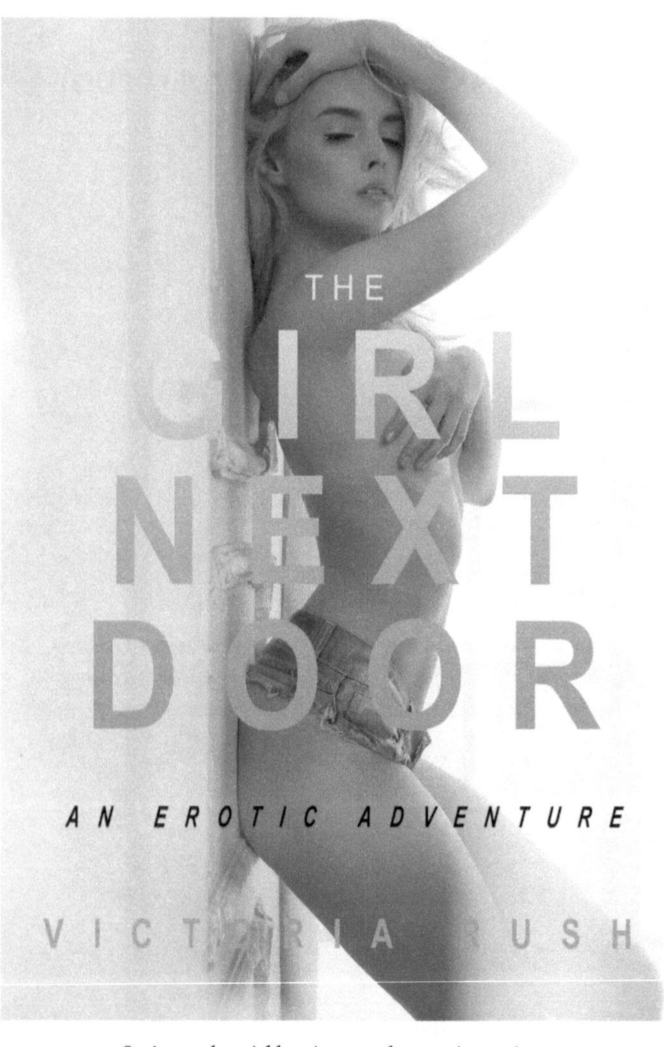

Spying on the neighbors just got a lot more interesting...

Everything's sexier in the dark...

NUDE CRUISE

AN EROTIC ADVENTURE

V I C T O R I A   R U S H

Some people get wet on a cruise for different reasons...

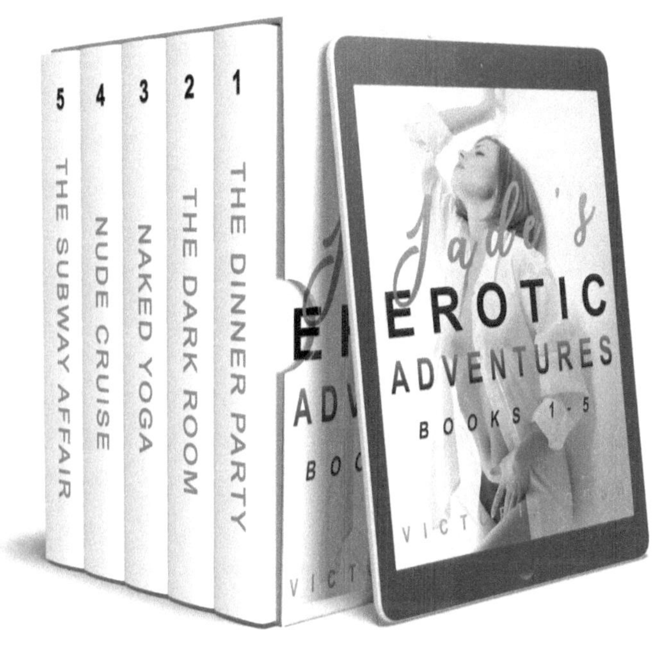

Books 1 -5 in the bestselling erotica series - 60% off

"Okay, so now that I'm committed, tell me where you had in mind for this little experiment."

"Actually," Hannah said, "I have a *series* of places in mind, each one more challenging than the one before."

"But I thought you said this was a one-off proposition?"

"I said nothing of the sort. I only said that if you won, I'd pay for the flights to Bora Bora. If you want me to cover the cost of hotels, food, and all the other incidentals, you'll have to pass progressively tougher tests. We don't want to make this *too* easy for you, do we?"

I crossed my arms and huffed, putting on my best pouty face.

"It hardly seems fair," I said. "But I'm still game. Besides, either one of us can pull out at any time to lock in our gains, right?"

"I suppose so," Hannah shrugged. "But what would be the fun in that? Something tells me once you've tried the first experiment, you won't want to stop. I think you're going to find this whole thing quite titillating and exciting. This will be the most fun either one of us has had in a long time."

I pushed the rest of my half-eaten salmon dish to the side, suddenly no longer interested in eating.

"Okay, lay it on me then. Where are you planning to take me for the first test?

Hannah gulped down the rest of her margarita then peered at me with a lopsided grin.

"Church. More specifically, a *Catholic* church. You haven't been in quite a while, have you? This will be your chance to repent and atone for all your sins."

"It's not like I've broken any commandments or anything–"

"The Catholic Church still considers sex outside of marriage a mortal sin. So technically, you've been doing a ton of sinning since your marriage ended."

"Well I haven't been a practicing Catholic for ages," I snorted. "So my conscience is clear. This'll be a cakewalk. All I have to do is sit quietly in my pew, right?"

"Yes, but it'll be a *front-row* pew, in full view of the priest who'll be delivering the sermon."

"Okay, but I'll be fully clothed, right? It's not like there'll be anything for him to see..."

"Not if you can keep your composure and don't cum all over the floor," Hannah said, cocking her head playfully.

"I don't think I'll have any difficulty keeping my dick in my pants, in a manner of speaking. But you raise a good point. You can't expect me not to get a little wet while you're stimulating me. What will I be allowed to wear?"

"I assume you'll dress appropriately, wearing your Sunday best. A mid-length skirt and button-up blouse should do the trick. You should be able to hide a few dribbles that way, right?"

"I suppose so, but how will we muffle the sound of the vibrator buzzing inside my panties? There's likely to be other people sitting around me in adjacent pews..."

"Never fear," Hannah smiled, reaching into her purse and pulling out a U-shaped silicone sex toy. "I've been talking with our friend at the local Babeland store. She's given me the latest prototype of the We-Vibe vibrator to test." She held up a smaller device with two control buttons and a flywheel. "Complete with a Bluetooth remote control. And the best thing is that it's whisper-quiet.

"Here," she said, handing me the flexible device. "See for yourself."

She tapped one of the buttons on the remote and the thick side of the contraption began buzzing softly in my hand.

"Okay," I nodded, looking around me to see if any other restaurant patrons were distracted by the gentle hum of the object. "It's *quiet* enough, but which end goes inside?"

"The bulbous end is a natural G-spot stimulator. You place the flatter end against your clit, then pull the thing up tight against your vulva to keep it snugly in place."

I suddenly became mindful of the wetness permeating my panties as I imagined the device vibrating inside me, surrounded by a bunch of oblivious bystanders.

"Can I give it a try here, like we did last time?" I grinned.

"No way," Hannah said, pulling the toy out of my hands. "There'll be no trial runs for this or any future tests. You'll just have to wait until we get to the church."

"And where will *you* be sitting while this is all going down?" I said.

"Right next to you, of course. I'll want a front-row seat to watch all the action."

On Sunday morning, Hannah picked me up and drove me the two miles to our local church. The entire time I squirmed in my seat trying to imagine what it would be like having a vibrator buzzing inside me in the quiet chapel. When we got to the church parking lot, she pulled into a sheltered space then plucked the blue vibrator out of her purse and handed it to me, resting her arm on the seat cushion expectantly.

"*What?*" I said. "You don't trust me to put it in privately?"

"Not really," she smirked. "For all I know, you might pull on some adult diapers under your skirt to hide any unintended releases. Here," she said, handing me a plastic vial. "I brought some lube to make it go in easier."

"I don't need any," I said, pulling the vibrator out of her hands and placing it under my skirt. "I'm already plenty worked up thinking about this scenario."

"I hope you're wearing panties under that skirt," Hannah said, watching me shift my weight as I placed the device against my vulva. "We wouldn't want it popping out at an inopportune moment."

"I'll just have to leave that up to your imagination," I sneered, lifting my skirt halfway up my thigh. "Unless you need to inspect the goods to make sure I'm not cheating."

"I trust you," Hannah smiled, opening her car door. "Something tells me you're looking forward to this just as much as I am."

As we approached the entrance to the church, I noticed a familiar figure standing at the top of the steps greeting the incoming parishioners, and he made eye contact with me when Hannah and I approached the landing.

"Jade!" Father Fife said, holding out his hands to me. "I haven't seen you in such a long time. It's so good to have you join us again."

"I'm sorry, Father," I said, placing my sweaty hand between his. "I've been a little distracted lately..."

"Life has a habit of getting in the way of the important things," he said. "We're just glad to have you whenever you can find time." He turned to Hannah, raising his eyebrows in curiosity. "And who's this lovely lady you've brought with you to attend our service today?"

"This is Hannah," I said, motioning toward my friend. "I thought I'd bring her along for moral support."

"Happy to have you, Hannah," Father Fife said, clasping Hannah's hands warmly. "The Lord knows we all need moral support wherever we can find it."

Hannah nodded politely, then the two of us walked through the entrance doors where I dipped my hand into the bowl of holy water and crossed my chest before continuing on toward the front of the chapel.

"*Jesus*," Hannah whispered, peering around the imposing shrine. "Is it just me, or did that feel a little creepy? All that talk about *having* us and that prolonged hand-holding. Hasn't he been paying any attention to the me-too movement?"

"I'm not sure any of that applies to men of the *cloth*," I chuckled. "But you better be careful about using the Lord's name like that around here. If anybody overhears you, you're liable to be burned at the stake."

The two of us stepped lively down the main aisle and finding a free spot in the front row, we took our seats flanked by two elderly couples. It was hard to imagine how Hannah would be able to use the remote-control device sandwiched so closely between other parishioners, and I crossed my legs, thankful for the brief respite. When everyone had filed into the chapel and the bell signaled the start of the service, a hush fell over the chamber and we all stood up as Father Fife walked onto the pulpit in his flowing robes.

"In the name of the Father, and of the Son, and of the Holy Spirit," he intoned solemnly.

"Amen," the congregation murmured in unison.

"The Lord be with you," he said.

"And with your spirit," the couples beside me retorted.

What the hell have I gotten myself into? I thought, feeling the flexible vibrator pressing against the inside of my closed legs. I didn't consider myself a terribly religious person, but being in this holy place surrounded by all the familiar rituals brought back all the old memories from my parents about the consequences of sinful behavior. *Surely getting secretly stimulated by a sex toy in the house of God will send me straight to hell.*

This was the point in the church service where everybody was supposed to take a moment to make a penitential act. While I listened to the other parishioners around me making their supplications, my knees began shaking as I made my own silent prayer for forgiveness.

"May Almighty God have mercy on us all," the priest said. "Forgive us our sins, and bring us to everlasting life."

"Amen," I joined in the congregation's response.

"Let us pray," Father Fife said, bowing his head.

As we closed our eyes and he began his opening prayer, Hannah nudged me with her knee and my mind raced with images of the pastor scornfully looking down at us while we played our blasphemous game. I peered up as he flapped his Bible closed, and caught him glancing in my direction.

"Through our Lord Jesus Christ, your Son," he said. "Who lives and reigns with you in the unity of the Holy Spirit, one God forever and ever."

"Amen," I said aloud, hoping he'd see me behaving like a good Catholic girl and turn his attention elsewhere.

He motioned for everyone to sit down and I was glad to get off my shaky feet onto the relative safety of the wooden pew.

"Good morning, ladies and gentlemen," he began his homily. "Today, I would like to talk with you about *morality*. Specifically, about the decaying state of society's morals in today's world. All around us we are surrounded by prurient symbols of modern decadence. First it was in the form of the printed word, then motion pictures, then the ubiquitous internet. It seems everywhere we turn, we are bombarded with profane and sacrilegious images."

I felt my heart pounding in my chest, like he was singling me out personally for my not-so-infrequent porn surfing.

"We seem to have forgotten," he railed, "the Lord's commandment that we shall not covet thy neighbor's wife. This admonition can be taken in its broadest context. Not only have many of you forsaken the sacred institution of marriage, but the egregious and widespread popularity of obscene *pornography* belies our unbridled lust and depravity. God slew Onan for spilling his seed, and so He will strike all others who practice self-abuse."

Hannah nudged her knee against mine, suddenly

reminding me why we were here. I was glad that she hadn't yet had the opportunity to take out her remote-control device, and I prayed that we'd be able to get through most of the service without her rudely interrupting it. I'd already begun to regret agreeing to this little venture, and I hoped that somehow we'd be able to bypass this first phase in her experiment.

"I'd like you to pick up your Bibles," Father Fife said, interrupting my thoughts. "And turn to Mark, Chapter 7, Verse 20."

Hannah and I reached down to pick up the bibles lying on the seat beside each of us, and we flipped to the indicated section.

"Read this passage with me, my friends," Father Fife instructed. "What comes *out* of a person is what defiles him," he enunciated, while the congregation quietly murmured along.

As I began to recite the passage along with him, I saw Hannah reach into her side pocket and place her closed hand between the book binding.

"For from within come evil thoughts," I continued reading as I peered out of the corner of my eye to see what she was up to.

"Sexual immorality, adultery, coveting, wickedness..." we read in unison.

Suddenly, I felt the interior end of the vibrator begin to tremble inside me and I stuttered, trying to finish the passage.

"Deceit...sensuality...envy..." I stammered, trying to catch my breath as I followed along. Hearing my labored recital, Hannah turned her head in my direction, acknowledging my silent suffering. She knew exactly what I was feeling and how difficult it was for me to remain composed as I read the script.

"All these evil things...come from *within*," I gulped as I began to feel the pleasure spread across my pelvic region. "And they defile a person."

"Consider these words carefully," the priest said, surveying my hunched-over posture. "For the Lord does not abide salacious thoughts and behavior. If you want passage into His Kingdom, you must be as pure and righteous as He."

He paused for a moment to let the message sink in, then he motioned with his two hands for us to be seated. I was grateful for the rest, and I froze upright in my chair trying to ignore the movement of the possessed instrument inside me.

"Let us consider for a moment *another* one of God's ten commandments," Father Fife continued. "Thou shall not commit *adultery*. The Lord made Eve from the flesh of Adam, and in so doing signified that forever more man shall be united to his wife as one..."

As Father Fife ramped up the intensity of his gayphobic critique, so did Hannah, furtively adjusting the flywheel on the remote-control device nestled under her palm in her lap. As she slowly increased the speed of the vibrations emanating inside my pussy, I squirmed on the bench, trying to restrain my rising passion.

"By rejecting the sanctity of marriage," Father Fife continued, glancing distractedly in my direction, "you have all *sinned*. In the book of Deuteronomy, we saw that God ordered adulterers be stoned to death. For your indiscriminate behavior, so shall the Lord indiscriminately smite thee."

Jesus, I thought. If that's what awaits a sinner for

cheating on their spouse, I wonder what happens to someone who self-abuses herself while sitting for Sunday Service in a house of God. *Surely I'll burn in hell for this act of sacrilege.*

Just when I thought I was beginning to get control over the delicious sensations stimulating my insides, Father Fife instructed us to stand once again and recite another passage from the Bible.

"Please stand now and read Peter 1:16 with me," he said.

Everyone stood and dutifully flipped to the relevant section of the scriptures. This time it was even harder for me to stand motionless, as my knees fluttered unsteadily from the pleasurable sensations radiating inside me.

"It is written..." I tried to read along. "That you shall be holy, for I am holy."

I saw Hannah's hands moving once again inside her prayer book, and suddenly I felt the *other* end of the U-shaped vibrator buzzing against my clit.

"And now Galatians 5:16," Father Fife instructed, barely giving me a chance to recover.

I flipped to the new citation and gasped for breath as my legs wobbled beneath me.

"But I say," I panted unsteadily. "Walk by the Spirit, and you will not gratify the desires of the flesh."

"So it is written," Father Fife said, closing his Bible. "Be righteous as the Lord, and you shall join him in Heaven for everlasting days. And now," he said, magnifying my torture. "I would like us to sing together one of my favorite hymns celebrating His blessing, *Amazing Grace*. Please pick up your hymn books and turn to page forty-three."

"Amazing grace, how sweet the sound," the priest began to sing as the entire congregation joined him in harmony.

"That saved a wretch like me," I sang along, trying to

ignore the message that seemed targeted directly at me. As I tried to hold the melody, Hannah cupped the remote-control device in her hand and turned the flywheel to its maximum setting.

"I once was lost, but now am found," I hyperventilated, pressing my legs together as hard as I could to stifle the rising passion that threatened to overtake me.

"Was blind, but now I see," I squealed, singing the last word decidedly off-pitch as Father Fife turned to see my entire body shaking as I belted the famous hymn.

By the time I'd finished the song, I'd somehow managed to keep it together and fight off the cresting passion that had threatened to put me over the edge. When we finally sat back down, Hannah mercifully turned the vibrator off, and I spread my hands over my ruffled skirt to signal that I'd managed to keep myself composed.

When the service was over and we walked up the aisle behind the rest of the assembly to exit the church, I couldn't wait to get out of the building to wash myself off, figuratively and literally. I was glad that we were at the back of the crowd so nobody could see the back of my skirt. I wasn't sure if my leaking pussy had left a stain, but I sure as hell didn't want one of the parishioners pointing it out. When we finally exited the entrance doors, Father Fife turned to the two of us and smiled.

"I noticed you seemed a little more passionate than usual reciting today's passages, Jade" he said to me.

"Yes, Father," I said, shaking his hand unsteadily. "I felt truly embodied by the spirit."

"And *you*, Hannah," he nodded. "Did you enjoy today's service also?"

"Oh yes," she said. "It was the most moving sermon I've attended in a long time."

"I hope you'll both come again," Father Fife said to the two of us.

"I'm sure we *will*, Father," Hannah smiled as we continued down the steps.

Like the second we get back home, I thought to myself, dying to tear off my clothes and squirt all over Hannah's face while she ate out my still-dripping pussy.

READ MORE...

ABOUT THE AUTHOR

If you would like to receive notification of new book(s) in Jade's Erotic Adventures, follow me at http://bookbub.com/authors/victoria-rush.

If you have a moment, please post a brief review on my Amazon book page at viewbook.at/thespa . Even just a couple of sentences will help other readers find and enjoy this book as much as you hopefully did.

Follow, share, like, and comment at:

www.facebook.com/authorvictoriarush
www.pinterest.com/authorvictoriarush
www.twitter.com/authorvictoriarush
authorvictoriarush@outlook.com

Hope to see you again soon!